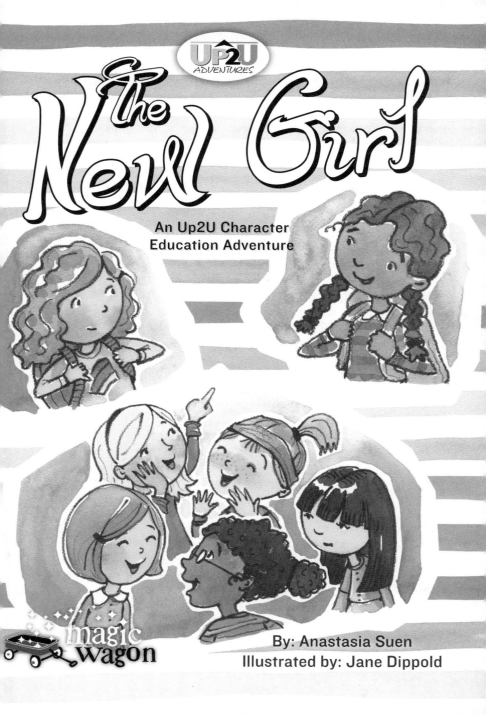

Up2U ADVENTURES

The New Girl

An Up2U Character Education Adventure

magic wagon

By: Anastasia Suen
Illustrated by: Jane Dippold

visit us at www.abdopublishing.com

Published by Magic Wagon, a division of the ABDO Group,
PO Box 398166, Minneapolis, MN 55439. Copyright © 2014 by
Abdo Consulting Group, Inc. International copyrights reserved
in all countries. All rights reserved. No part of this book may
be reproduced in any form without written permission from the
publisher.

Calico Chapter Books™ is a trademark and logo of Magic Wagon.

Printed in the United States of America, North Mankato, Minnesota.
052013
092013
♲ This book contains at least 10% recycled materials.

Written by Anastasia Suen
Illustrated by Jane Dippold
Edited by Stephanie Hedlund and Rochelle Baltzer
Cover and interior design by Neil Klinepier

Library of Congress Cataloging-in-Publication Data
Suen, Anastasia.
  The new girl : an Up2U character education adventure / by
Anastasia Suen ; illustrated by Jane Dippold.
    p. cm. -- (Up2U adventures)
  Summary: Vanessa is the new girl in class, and Sara is torn between
sympathy, because she knows what being teased is like, and a desire
to stay with the "in" crowd led by Courtney, chief bully, and the
reader is invited to choose between three possible choices for Sara to
make.
  ISBN 978-1-61641-968-4
  1. Plot-your-own stories. 2. Bullying--Juvenile fiction. 3.
Interpersonal relations--Juvenile fiction. 4. Friendship--Juvenile
fiction. 5. Schools--Juvenile fiction. [1. Bullies--Fiction. 2.
Interpersonal relations--Fiction. 3. Friendship--Fiction. 4. Schools--
Fiction. 5. Plot-your-own stories.] I. Dippold, Jane, ill. II. Title.
  PZ7.S94343New 2013
  813.6--dc23
                          2013001730

Table of Contents

Oh, No, You Don't

Pigtails. That was the first thing I noticed. The new girl had pigtails. Her hair was thick and black. It was really beautiful, actually. The only problem was, she was wearing it up in pigtails.

I used to wear my hair in pigtails. But I don't wear them to school anymore. Instead, I wear my hair long. It is way past my shoulders now. I'm used to wearing it down. I even started liking it that way.

Which is good, because Courtney doesn't like pigtails. Courtney is the most popular girl in the fifth grade. She looks like a model with her long, blonde hair. It isn't as long as mine and it is straight, not curly like mine.

Courtney is pretty and popular, but she isn't nice. Everyone does what she says, or she gets

4

mad. You don't want to see her when she is mad. It isn't pretty. She scrunches up her face and looks all mean. So, we all try to keep her happy.

"Come in," said Mrs. Case. "Welcome to Room 7."

"This is Vanessa Gomez," said Principal Thatcher.

"Pigtails!" hissed Courtney. "Can you believe it?"

Jessica, Ashley, and Lexi started snickering. Whatever Courtney said, they did.

I looked over at Grace. She is my best friend. Grace has long black hair like Vanessa does, but she never wears it in pigtails. Never. Grace had been there when I wore pigtails to school. That was way back in the third grade. It was my first year at Meadows, and I didn't know all of Courtney's rules yet. But I found out in a hurry.

Grace looked at Courtney and shook her head. She doesn't like it when Courtney is mean. I don't either. Why should something as little as pigtails cause someone to be so mean anyway?

"Why don't you sit here," said Mrs. Case.

I looked up. Mrs. Case was standing right next to me. There was an open desk right next to her. No one ever sat in that chair. I just used it to keep my backpack off the floor.

"I, uh . . ." I stood up and picked up my backpack. Now someone could sit in the chair.

"Thanks," said Vanessa. She sat down.

Courtney and her followers had their heads together. I couldn't hear what they were saying. Lexi pointed at Vanessa and they all started laughing.

"Now, now," said Mrs. Case. "Where is that extra math book?" She walked over to the

shelves at the back of the class. She turned her back to the class as she crouched down to look at the books.

I looked over at Vanessa. She was looking down at her desk. Everyone was talking about her and she knew it.

Courtney reached up and pulled her long hair into pretend pigtails. Then she made a grunting sound. Everyone laughed, even the boys.

Mrs. Case stood up. "What?" she asked the class.

Courtney had her hands on her desk now. She looked innocent. The teachers never knew how mean she was to everyone else.

Mrs. Case turned back to the shelf. "I know it has to be here somewhere." She knelt down next to the shelf.

I looked over at Vanessa. She was taking

out her pigtails, first one and then the other. She put the hair bands on her wrist. Then she opened her backpack and took out her brush.

"Psst!" said Grace. She pointed at Courtney.

Courtney was pretending to brush her hair. But the look on her face was just awful. She held her chin up and closed her eyes. She was acting like she was a beauty queen. This made the class laugh even louder.

"Settle down," said Mrs. Case. She stood up and brushed her hands together. "I just can't find it." She walked over to Vanessa.

"You can share books with Sara for now," said Mrs. Case.

Who, me? I looked up at Mrs. Case. "Okay," I muttered.

"You're such a nice girl, Sara," said Mrs. Case. Then she walked to the front of the room. "Okay, class, open your math books to page 157. You'll need a pencil and paper, too."

There was a flurry of activity as everyone got ready for math. Finally, we could stop looking at the new girl. I remembered how terrible that felt.

Courtney turned and looked at me. She puckered her lips, three times in a row.

A kiss up? Courtney thought I was a kiss up?

It wasn't like I had a choice. But I knew what was coming next. Courtney didn't like it when someone else got attention. She wanted to be in the spotlight at all times. If you took that away from her, she always got back at you . . . somehow.

Jumped

Scraape! Vanessa pushed her desk next to mine. I mean, they were touching and everything.

"There, that's better. Now I can see the book," said Vanessa.

Everyone in the class turned around to look. I was starting to get uncomfortable.

"Good thinking, Sara," Mrs. Case finally said.

Courtney glared at me. I was the center of attention again. She didn't like that, not one bit. I knew trouble would be coming my way later.

Grace turned her head sideways as if to ask, *what are you doing?*

But, I didn't do anything. I couldn't do anything! Mrs. Case was looking at me, too. I had to act like everything was okay, but it wasn't.

You see, I used to sit next to Grace. Then, Mrs. Case moved her. She said that we talked too much when our desks were next to one another. Well, that was what best friends did. They talked all the time.

I didn't understand why this was okay now. When the new girl moved her desk next to mine it was "good thinking"? No wonder Grace was confused. I was confused, too. And I wanted everyone to stop staring at me.

"Alright class, back to fractions. As you can see on this page . . .," Mrs. Case continued the lesson. Finally, the rest of the class turned back around and we got to work.

After math was over, I thought everything would go back to normal. But Mrs. Case couldn't find the language arts book either. So Vanessa's desk stayed right next to mine. She didn't even move when we wrote in our daily writing logs. I didn't think she needed to sit so close to do that, but she didn't move her desk at all.

I tried to stay calm. I didn't say anything. I thought over my options. But, I couldn't move my desk away without bumping into Tyler. If I did that, he would say something and everyone would turn around again. I didn't want everyone staring again.

We had social studies next and of course, there was no book. That's what happens when you start school in the middle of the day, in the middle of the year. No one is ready for you.

So the new girl's desk stayed next to mine. It was just like glue, stuck forever. Just like all of those stares I was getting from Courtney.

She glared at me every time a book couldn't be found.

It wasn't my fault there weren't any books. Why did I have to be in the middle of it? I used to like sitting here by the window. If I couldn't talk to Grace at least I could see all of the little pink flowers. Pink was my favorite color.

"Do you have any more paper?" Vanessa asked politely.

I looked up. Mrs. Case was watching me again. She nodded at me. I guess that meant yes. Go ahead and give the new girl some paper.

I nodded back. I didn't want to say anything. I didn't want anyone else to turn around and stare. So I opened up my notebook and tore out three sheets of paper. That should be enough for the rest of the day. Then she would leave me alone.

I just wanted everyone to leave me alone. I looked up at the clock. This day was taking forever! It wasn't even time for lunch yet. *Tick, tick, tick!* I stared at the clock, willing the hands to move. *Hurry up and move faster, clock.* But that didn't help at all. In fact, time slowed down as I waited to be free.

Ring! Finally! I jumped up and unzipped my backpack. I took out my lunch and walked toward the door. I had to get out of the room now. I couldn't take any more of Courtney's stares.

"Wait up," Vanessa called to me.

Now what? I thought. *I've shared books and given you my paper. What else could you possibly want?*

I looked over and saw Grace walking out the door. If I hurried, I could catch up with her instead of being trapped with the new girl.

"Grace," I called out. She kept walking. So I said it louder, "Grace!"

Grace didn't even look back. She ran over to Lexi and started talking. What was all that about?

"Which way is the lunchroom?" said Vanessa.

I pointed down the hallway. Everyone was walking that way. It was so obvious.

"What are we waiting for?" Vanessa asked. "Let's go."

Excuse me? I don't even know you, I thought. I stared at Vanessa. Then Mrs. Case came out of the classroom.

"Oh, good, you're together," said Mrs. Case. "Sara, can you take Vanessa to the lunchroom and show her around? I have to go to the office. We need to find her some books."

"Thank you, Mrs. Case," said Vanessa.

Just like that, I was trapped again. There was nothing I could do. I wanted to make my teacher happy. I couldn't be rude. So, I smiled and nodded. Then I walked down the hallway with Vanessa.

We entered the lunchroom together. But I wasn't paying attention to Vanessa at all. Instead I was scanning the room for Grace. I spotted her pretty quickly. She was sitting at Courtney's table next to Lexi. That was strange. We always sat together at lunch.

I walked over to their table. "Hi, Grace," I said and put my lunch on the table.

"Oh, no, you don't," Courtney sneered, stopping me in my tracks. "You may not sit at our table."

"Grace," I said. But she was looking the other way. Even my best friend wouldn't talk to me.

Now what? I wondered.

"Let's sit over there," Vanessa suggested. She pointed at the third graders' tables. They were on the other side of the lunchroom. But, there was plenty of room over there.

Sure, why not? Today was just like third grade all over again. I picked up my lunch and walked away.

Moving On

"Bye, Mom!" I got out of the car and closed the door. It was a new day. Things were going to be better today.

Grace was up ahead of me. I was worrying about her all night. I even called, but she never called me back. I didn't call that late, but Grace's mom had all kinds of rules about school nights. Oh well, we could talk now.

"Grace!" I called out. But she didn't turn around. She just walked into the office like she hadn't heard me. I was kind of far away, so maybe she didn't hear me yell. I quickly walked over to the office and followed her inside.

When I walked through the door, I found Grace holding the flag. It was folded into a triangle. I had forgotten this was Grace's week for flag duty. Everyone in the fifth grade was in charge of raising and lowering the flag at least once during the school year. I had my week the month before.

Everyone works in pairs for flag duty. I had put the flag up with Courtney. She was nice to me then. That was probably because I had let her carry the flag and pull the rope. Courtney liked it when she was in charge.

"Grace!" I said again. I was closer this time, and I knew she could hear me. But, she still didn't turn around. Now I had the feeling something must be wrong. I wanted to talk to Grace to find out what I had done to make her mad at me.

I wondered who was helping Grace with flag duty. Maybe I could help her. I didn't see any other fifth graders in the office. I was just about to offer to help her—and then I saw the red hair. It was Lexi, one of Courtney's friends, or should I say Courtney's followers. Lexi did whatever Courtney said.

Lexi and Grace started walking out of the office right toward me. This was my chance.

"Hi, Grace," I said. She didn't look at me. She was staring at the floor with a frown on her face. Then she and Lexi walked past me as if I wasn't there.

I stared at them. I couldn't believe my best friend would ignore me like that. It was all because of the new girl, and I hadn't even seen her yet today.

Lexi and Grace skipped out the front door to the flagpole. I couldn't watch them anymore. I turned and walked the other way. I had to be in class before the bell rang. I didn't need to be late and have any more trouble.

What's next? I wondered, as I walked down the hall. I didn't have to wait long for the answer. Courtney was blocking the classroom doorway. Jessica and Ashley were right beside her.

When Courtney saw me, she puckered her lips and made a kissing sound. Jessica and Ashley laughed. Courtney was calling me a kiss up again.

What could I say? Nothing. So, I just walked past them. I didn't want to give them a reaction. My mom said that was what bullies wanted.

Courtney didn't like that one bit. She followed me into the classroom. I quickly looked over at Mrs. Case. Courtney did too.

Mrs. Case was talking to another student. Her back was turned toward us. She couldn't see anything that was going on. That was all that Courtney needed. She pulled her hair into pigtails. "Oink!" she snorted.

Not again! I looked over at Vanessa. The new girl was sitting at her desk. It was still next to mine. But Vanessa wasn't wearing pigtails. Neither was I.

"Oink! Oink!" repeated Jessica and Ashley.

Ring! Thank goodness it was time for school to start. Maybe Courtney and her friends would find something else to do now.

"Seats, everyone," said Mrs. Case. "It's time to take roll."

Just as Mrs. Case finished her sentence, Grace and Lexi came in the door.

"The flag is up," Grace announced.

"It's nice and high," Lexi added.

"Thank you, ladies," said Mrs. Case. Then she looked at me. "Isn't it your week to take roll, Sara?" she asked.

With all my worries about Grace and Courtney, I had forgotten about roll call! I stood up and walked to the front of the class.

Courtney made a hissing sound as I walked past. So of course Jessica, Ashley, and Lexi hissed, too.

"Settle down, class," said Mrs. Case. "It's time for morning announcements."

I took out the roll sheet and looked at the desks. There was an empty seat in the third row. That was Dylan's desk. I marked him as absent next to his name.

I had been at this school since the third grade, so I knew everyone. Well, everyone except Vanessa, but I knew her name. That was all I needed to take roll.

I knew who was who. I knew who I could trust. I also knew that Courtney wouldn't stop until she got what she wanted—to be the center of attention. But when would all of the attention go back to her? There was a new girl here now and that changed everything.

Courtney wasn't really my friend. She just pretended to be when she wanted something. Courtney liked having lots of followers. Well, I wasn't going to follow her anymore. No way. Vanessa needed a friend.

I looked over at my best friend Grace. She saw me looking and turned away.

It looked like I needed a new friend now, too.

Lies

So here we were, sitting at the third grade tables for lunch again. Just me and Vanessa. It was like I was in third grade all over again. Back when Courtney didn't like me. And now, well, she didn't like me anymore again.

I looked over at Vanessa. She was eating her lunch and not saying a word. I knew why. No one had said anything nice to her since she had come to this school. And what had she done wrong? She had worn pigtails. Really? Was that so wrong? She looked cute in them.

I looked over at the fifth grade tables. Just two days ago I had been sitting there with my best friend. Now she was sitting next to Lexi. And Lexi was sitting next to Courtney, of course. Jessica and Ashley were sitting on

the other side. Courtney was always the center of attention. She would have it no other way.

Courtney said something and they all started laughing, except Grace. She had a strange look on her face. She stared at the table as she slowly ate her lunch.

What is going on? Are they talking about me? I wondered.

Courtney pointed at me and laughed.

I knew it. They are talking about me. I looked away.

Why wouldn't Courtney just leave me alone? I was leaving her alone. I was here with the new girl, who wasn't saying anything either. Not a word. We were sitting all the way over here on the other side of the cafeteria in silence.

And then I heard it. "Sara likes Ethan."

Ethan was the cutest boy in the class. Every girl in the class liked him, even Grace. I looked over at my best friend.

Grace was looking back at me this time. She had a surprised look on her face. Then she quickly looked at Courtney.

Grace told Courtney! I thought. *How could you, Grace? How could you tell them that I liked Ethan? You promised to keep it a secret. Why did you lie? Why didn't you tell them that you liked him, too?*

When Grace glanced back at me, I shook my head at her. Grace quickly looked down at her lunch. It was as if I wasn't there at all.

"Sara likes Ethan?" said Jessica. "Oh, that's a good one!" And then they all laughed.

Courtney turned and looked at me. She knew that I was watching her. She knew that I was listening. She stood up and walked to the end of the fifth grade tables. That was where all the boys sat.

"Have you heard?" she asked.

"What?" said Ryan.

"Sara likes Ethan," said Courtney.

"What?" Ethan asked. He was sitting on the other side of the table. His back was toward me, so I couldn't see his face.

Courtney walked around the table. She stood next to Ethan and looked right at me. "I said I heard Sara likes you."

I held my breath. What would Ethan say? I didn't think I could stand it anymore.

"Sara!" said Ethan. He looked around at all of the other kids at the table watching him. Then he laughed. So, of course, all of the other kids laughed, too. Courtney was right there in the middle of it all, laughing at me.

When they heard the laughing, the other girls came over and stood next to Courtney. Everyone was looking at her as she talked. She was the center of attention again, just the way she liked it.

I looked over at Grace. She was the only one of the group that didn't join Courtney. Now, she was just sitting there, staring at the table as she ate her lunch. In that moment, I knew she didn't care about me at all. My best friend had dumped me.

I was still confused. Why had Grace told Courtney that? Why did I tell Grace in the first place? I thought she was my best friend, but that was a lie.

Suddenly I wasn't hungry anymore. I put the apple back in my lunch bag. I had to get out of this place. I wasn't going to just sit there and listen to them talk about me.

"Come on, Vanessa," I said. "Let's go."

"Okay," she said.

We stood up and walked out of the cafeteria.

A New Day

Wednesday, it was Wednesday already. I lay in bed with my eyes closed. I didn't want to wake up and start the day.

So far it had been a terrible week. Things hadn't been this bad, well, since I had been the new girl.

But yesterday, after she humiliated me, Courtney was finally happy. She didn't bother me for the rest of the day. She ignored me. And that was okay. Being ignored was better than being bullied.

So what was I going to do? I thought about it as I got dressed, as I ate breakfast, and as I got out of the car at school. What was I going to do?

"Bye, Mom!" I said.

"Bye," said Mom. "Have a nice day."

That was it. I was going to have a nice day. I closed the door and waved good-bye. Then I turned to face the school.

I was going to have a nice day, just like I always did. I would act like nothing happened. Even if it killed me.

On my way into school, I had to walk past the flagpole. The flag wasn't up yet. I went into the school and looked at the office as I passed. Grace was in there with Lexi. They were talking to Mrs. Thatcher about something.

I walked down the hallway and then into class. No one said anything to me. No kissing, no oinking, no pointing. So far it was a good morning.

I walked over to my desk and took off my backpack. Vanessa wasn't here yet, but her desk was piled high with books. Wait!

What? Vanessa had her own books! No more sharing? Hooray! And her desk was back where it belonged. Mrs. Case must have moved it.

"Courtney!" someone called out. I was afraid to look up, but I did. Just then, Ashley ran over to Courtney. Jessica was right behind her. They were looking at each other's fingers.

"It changes colors," said Ashley.

I looked at Ashley's hand. She was wearing a mood ring. The stone on those rings changes colors when your mood changes. If I had one of those rings right now, the color would've changed from black to blue. I wasn't stressed out anymore. I was happy. Courtney and her friends were going to leave me alone today.

While Courtney and her group were gaping at their rings, Vanessa came in. She looked at her desk and grinned.

"My books came!" She sat down and opened them one by one.

Vanessa didn't need me anymore. I was glad. Maybe now things would go back to normal.

"Hey, Ryan," said Ethan.

This time I didn't look. I just couldn't. I turned my head and listened instead.

"I can't believe you missed that pitch," said Ryan.

"Yeah, yeah," said Ethan, "like you always hit the ball. I saw you strike out yesterday."

"Now wait a minute," said Ryan. "That pitcher was—"

"Too fast," said Ethan. "I know. I was there."

Baseball. They were talking about baseball. Not me, not yesterday at lunch. I relaxed again. It has to all be over now.

"Let me see," said Lexi. I turned my head just a bit. Lexi ran over to Ashley. Ashley was holding out her hand. Courtney had hers out, too. She always had to be the center of attention. They were still talking about rings.

Where was Grace? I looked around the room. There she was taking the books out of her backpack. She was nowhere near Courtney. Grace was back to being Grace.

Ring! It was time for class.

Grace turned and looked at me. I smiled. She smiled back.

If I was wearing my mood ring right now, it would have just turned purple. I was very happy. It was going to be a great day.

Choosing Sides

"Ooh, it's JJ," said Courtney as we walked into the gym for PE.

Oh no, not him. Not Mr. Jackson. Our regular teacher was Coach G. But his wife had a new baby the day before, so he wasn't there.

"JJ is so handsome," said Courtney. Ashley, Jessica, and Lexi started giggling.

I didn't like Mr. Jackson. Not one bit.

All the boys liked him because he had played pro basketball. Or so he said. I've never heard of any of his teams.

"They call me Jump Jackson," he told us the first time we met him. "JJ for short." And then he jumped up. Well, he was tall and he could jump very high. But if he was so good at basketball, why was he here? Why wasn't he out playing sports with the grown-ups?

"Okay, kids," said JJ. "Line up against the wall."

"What are we going to do today, JJ?" asked Courtney.

I knew what he was going to say. The only thing we ever did when JJ came—play dodgeball. I hated dodgeball. All you did was hit people with the ball. That wasn't a real sport.

"Do you guys want to play some dodgeball?" asked JJ.

"Yeah," yelled the boys.

Of course the boys loved dodgeball. It gave them a chance to hit people—and not get in trouble.

"Line up against the wall," said JJ. "We need to choose teams."

"Yeah," said Ryan. He gave Ethan a high five.

As we lined up, JJ looked us over. He had to choose team captains. I knew who he would choose. He chose the same people every time.

"I choose . . .," said JJ, acting like he was thinking hard. Finally, he pointed at Ethan. "You!"

Ethan strutted across the gym and stood in the center of the court.

Then JJ walked over by the girls. Courtney touched her long, blonde hair and smiled at him.

"And you," said JJ. He pointed at Courtney.

"Me?" said Courtney, like it was a surprise. Then she walked over and stood next to Ethan.

JJ joined them at the center of the court. "Now we have to choose our teams." He put his hand on Courtney's shoulder. "Ladies first."

Courtney giggled. Then she looked at the girls lined up against the wall. "I choose Jessica."

No surprise there. Courtney always chose Jessica first. Jessica ran over and stood next to Courtney.

JJ put his hand on Ethan's shoulder. "Now you, sport," said JJ.

Ethan pointed at Ryan. Ryan nodded and slowly walked over.

"Now you, little lady," said JJ.

Courtney and Jessica both giggled. Then Courtney pointed at Ashley.

One by one Ethan and Courtney each chose a new person. In less than a minute, I was the only one standing against the wall.

"A leftover?" said JJ, pointing at me.

Oh great, now I was a leftover.

"Wait a minute," said JJ. "How many kids are in your class?" He counted out loud. "1, 2, 3 . . . 35? Thirty-five," he repeated. "How did that happen?"

Vanessa came, that's what happened. And now we were an uneven number. Seventeen and seventeen were thirty-four, and I was the remainder, the leftover. Number thirty-five.

"Sorry, kid," JJ said. "You'll just have to sit this one out. It wouldn't be fair to let you play."

And then he turned his back to me. He left me standing by the wall, by myself. What was I supposed to do for the full gym hour?

"Okay, kids," said JJ. "Let's play some dodgeball."

And so they did. They started playing dodgeball without me. They threw the ball and laughed and shouted. No one even looked at me, not even Grace.

Ethan didn't choose me like he always did, and I knew why. Grace had told Courtney that I liked Ethan. When I was the center of attention because of Vanessa, Courtney wanted to get back at me. So she told Ethan in front of everyone. The whole class knew.

I thought Ethan had forgotten. He hadn't said anything that morning. But he didn't forget. He chose Vanessa instead of me. He chose the new girl for his team. Ethan didn't like me, not one bit. I knew that and now everyone in the class knew, too. It was the worst day of my life.

Raising the Flag

The next day I was back in the carpool line at school. The cars slowly moved forward. What did that bumper sticker say? Pass it on.

I'd rather pass it by. If I had my way, we would keep driving and never come back. I didn't want to go to this school anymore.

But I didn't say anything to Mom. I didn't want her to ask any questions. So I just sat there.

Finally, we reached the front of the line. The carpool monitor opened the door for me. I got out of the car just like I did every other day.

I closed the car door and waved at Mom. I acted happy on the outside. How could I tell her that my best friend wasn't . . . well, wasn't even my friend anymore?

I watched as she drove away. Then I turned and looked at the school. I used to like coming to school. That was back when I had friends. We had a good time here. But now, everyone hated me. It was terrible.

I rounded the corner and saw Grace alone at the flagpole. Lexi wasn't in sight. Grace was trying to raise the flag all by herself. It was draped over her shoulder.

Grace was trying to put a hook into the hole at the top of the flag. It was right next to the stars. But it wasn't working. The hook wasn't going in and the flag was slipping off her shoulder.

I ran over and picked up the edge of the flag. "Let me help," I said. The rule was that the flag wasn't supposed to touch the ground. I knew that. I'd had flag duty the month before with Ethan. Back when he was talking to me. That was before Grace…

"Thanks!" said Grace.

I held the flag while Grace put in the first hook. *Click!*

Grace pulled the rope to lift up the top half of the flag. *Scree, scree!*

Now it was time for the second hook. I moved the flag in closer. Grace put in the bottom hook. *Click!*

I held on to the flag as Grace pulled the rope. *Scree, scree, scree, scree!* The flag lifted out of my hands. It went higher and higher until it reached the top of the pole. Then it began to flap in the breeze.

Grace wrapped the bottom of the rope around the hook. That would keep the flag flying. Grace moved the rope back and forth, making a figure eight around the hook. Then she looped the last bit of rope around the top. We were done. Now the flag would fly all day.

After school we would . . . Wait, where was Lexi? It was her week to help Grace, not mine. Why wasn't Lexi helping Grace with the flag? What was going on? Did I really want to know?

I looked at Grace. I wondered what she would say now.

"Thanks," said Grace. "I thought I could do it by myself."

"Some things are hard to do alone," I said. "Sometimes you need a friend."

I wasn't just talking about the flag. I didn't like it when everyone ignored me or made fun of me. It was all because of what Grace told Courtney.

I couldn't take it anymore. I looked Grace in the eye and asked her point-blank, "Why did you tell Courtney that I liked Ethan?"

She blinked. "I didn't. I didn't say a word. I promise. I would never do that to you, Sara," she said.

"Then how did she know?" I asked.

Grace waved her hands. "Everyone likes Ethan," said Grace, "especially Courtney. She likes him the most."

Now it was my turn to blink in confusion. "Oh, I didn't know that."

I looked at the flowers growing behind us. The pink blossoms were so pretty. I watched as one fluttered down to the ground.

If Grace didn't tell, then why did she ignore me all week? Why didn't she return my call? Why didn't she look at me in class? Why didn't she sit by me at lunch? Something wasn't right.

"Grace," I said, "I know something is going on. You haven't been yourself. You know you can tell me anything. What is wrong?"

"Ooba-chan," said Grace. Her eyes filled with tears.

I put my hand on Grace's shoulder.

"What is it?" I asked gently.

Tears were running down Grace's cheeks. "My grandmother," said Grace. "My grandmother is very sick. She might . . ." Grace shook her head.

"Oh, Grace!" I put my arms around her. "I'm so sorry. Why didn't you tell me?"

"I don't want to think about it," said Grace. "I don't . . ."

"Okay," I said. I let go of her. "Let's talk about something else."

Grace rubbed the tears off her face. "Okay, what?"

"Well," I said, "what am I going to do about Vanessa? Courtney hates it when I talk to her. But Vanessa didn't do anything to Courtney. She's just the new girl. I was the new girl once, too. I know how it feels."

"I don't know," said Grace. "What do you want to do?"

What am I going to do now? Well, that was the question of the day. What did I really want?

The Ending is Up2U!

If you want Sara to ignore Vanessa and make friends with Courtney, go to page 55.

If you want Sara to be polite to Vanessa, go to page 62.

If you want Sara to make friends with Vanessa, go to page 71.

Ending 1: Old Friends

I looked at Grace. She looked back. She was still my friend. Her grandmother was sick, that was the problem. That was why she was ignoring me. She didn't hate me like everyone else did. She was just upset about her grandmother. I knew what that was like. It was scary when someone you loved got sick. What if she died?

I shook my head. No, no, no. I wasn't going to think about that. My grandmother got better. Grace's grandmother would get better, too.

"We have to go to class," said Grace.

"Okay," I said. We walked into the building together. The hallway was crowded. Everyone was rushing to class. No one noticed me. It was just like any other day.

I've been at this school for a long time. Back when I was new, it took a while to get Courtney to talk to me. Popular people can be so picky sometimes. What Courtney wants, Courtney gets. If she doesn't like it when I help Vanessa, then I'll stop.

I have to. Look at what happened when I didn't do what she said. Courtney turned on me.

Grace and I walked past the cafeteria. I had to sit on the other side of the cafeteria with the third graders. But why? I'm not in the third grade anymore.

And that didn't make Courtney stop. Even when I sat over there with the new girl, Courtney still hated me. She told everyone that I liked Ethan—and now Ethan won't even talk to me.

It's just not right.

One new girl comes to school and now I'm the one they don't like? I only shared my books because Mrs. Case made me.

When Grace and I walked into class, I looked around the room. Vanessa was sitting at her desk. She was still the new girl, but she had her own books now. Mrs. Case didn't need me to help her anymore. It was over.

I don't have to sit on the other side of the cafeteria at lunch anymore. I don't have to be the new girl's friend. I have my own friend.

I looked over at Grace. We had been friends for a long, long time. I wanted things to go back to the way they were. Let Vanessa find her own friends. If I ignored Vanessa, Courtney would like me again.

If I acted like I always did, Courtney would stop talking about me. That's what I was going to do now. I would just act like nothing happened.

"Hey Courtney," I said, "is Lexi okay?"

Courtney looked up at me. What would she say now?

"Yeah, she's okay," said Courtney. "She just had to get new bands on her braces."

Lexi had gotten braces on her teeth a few months ago. She always wore brightly colored bands on them. All of Courtney's friends wore the same color bands. Last month, they all had blue ones. The month before, it was yellow.

"I wonder what color she will get this time," I said.

"Hey, Jessica," said Courtney, "smile for Sara."

Jessica smiled. She had bright orange bands on her braces.

"Orange," I said, "just right for Halloween."

Courtney nodded. "I get mine after school. It's so nice when everyone matches."

I nodded and smiled. So that was it. She liked it when everyone is the same. If you were different, then she got upset.

Well, I was going to be the same as I always was. I just talked to her like nothing was wrong, and she didn't tease me at all.

Ring! "Seats, everyone," said Mrs. Case.

I walked over and sat down just like any other day. I didn't even look at Vanessa. If I acted like she wasn't here, everything would be just fine.

Vanessa tried to talk to me when Mrs. Case wasn't looking. I wouldn't look at her or reply. I felt bad, but I had to do what was best for me.

As the weeks went by, Vanessa stopped trying to talk to me. Courtney went back to normal. Ethan even picked me for dodgeball the next time JJ was the substitute. My life was back to normal.

But for some reason I still felt bad. Watching Vanessa eat lunch alone didn't help. But, I couldn't upset Courtney again. It's just the way it has to be.

Ending 2: Just Be Nice

What am I going to do? What else could I do? I had to be polite to everyone. That's just who I was.

It wasn't my fault that Courtney was rude. She always acted that way. But that didn't mean that I had to be rude, too.

I looked at Grace. She looked back. She was still my friend. Her grandmother was sick, that was the problem. That was why she was ignoring me. She didn't hate me like everyone else did. She was just upset about her grandmother. I knew what that was like.

It was scary when someone you loved got sick. What if she died?

I shook my head. No, no, no. I wasn't going to think about that. My grandmother got better. Grace's grandmother would get better too.

"We have to go to class," said Grace.

I opened the front door to the school for Grace and we both walked in. I waved at Mrs. Thatcher in the office as we walked past.

Yes, that was the only way. I had to be me, no matter what.

I looked over at Grace. I was so happy that she was still my friend. We had been friends for so long, ever since I came to this school.

I wish I had known about her grandmother before. I would have worried a lot less if I had known. I could have helped her, too. But I understood. She didn't want to talk about it. I knew what that was like.

I remember how afraid I was when my grandmother got sick. I didn't want to talk about it either.

We turned the corner and walked by the cafeteria. I wasn't going to sit with the third graders anymore. No, today I would sit with Grace, just like I always did. If Vanessa wanted to sit with the third grade, that was fine with me. It was her choice. But I wanted to sit with my best friend again.

Grace and I walked into class. I looked around. Lexi wasn't there.

"Where is Lexi?" I asked Grace.

Grace shrugged. "I don't know."

"I hope Lexi is okay," I said.

"It's no fun to be sick," said Grace. She frowned as she sat down at her desk. She must

be thinking about her grandmother again.

"Let me ask Courtney," I said. "She'll know."

I walked over to Courtney's desk. "Where is Lexi?" I asked. "She wasn't here to help Grace with the flag. Is everything okay?"

Courtney waved her hand. She had a new color of nail polish. Yesterday she was wearing blue but today it was orange. Halloween was coming up. That must be why.

"Lexi will be here later," said Courtney. "She just had to go to the orthodontist."

"Oh," I said. I had forgotten about that. I didn't have braces, but everyone else did.

"Jessica," said Courtney, "show Sara your bands."

Jessica smiled. Her mouth was filled with braces and orange rubber bands.

"Lexi will get orange," said Courtney, "and

so will I. It's so nice when everyone matches." She waved her orange fingernails again.

So that was it. I looked over at Jessica. Her nails were orange, too. They were all going to match. Everyone was wearing orange for Halloween.

I nodded and smiled. I wasn't just being polite. I really did like it when everything fit together. That was why this week had been so upsetting. I didn't like it when I didn't fit in. I didn't like it when no one would talk to me.

"When you get your braces," said Courtney, "you will match, too."

Oh, wow. That was a big change. Why was Courtney being nice to me now? Was it just because I was talking to her about her?

She took my hand and looked at my nails. "You only have on clear polish? You have to try this orange." She turned my hand over so I could see her nails instead.

"It is a nice color," I said.

Jessica came over and showed me her nails. Ashley stood right beside her. They all had the same nail polish.

"I'll have to get some," I said.

"Yes, you should," said Courtney.

And just like that, Courtney was talking to me again. No kissing sounds, no pig noises, no telling my secrets in public. It was as if Vanessa had never come. Everything was forgotten.

So what changed? I listened as they talked about putting on the polish. Ashley had only put on one coat of polish. Courtney insisted that two coats were better. Jessica agreed right away. Courtney smiled at her.

That was it. When I came over to see her, I made her the center of attention. I asked about one of her friends. I agreed with her about the polish. I let her tell me what to do. She liked that.

I didn't do it to make Courtney like me. I did it because I was worried about Lexi. And I didn't lie either. I really did like the nail polish. Who knew that being polite would solve the problem?

I looked over at Vanessa. She had her own books now. She didn't need me to take care of her anymore. I would be polite to her, too. Why not? It was the right thing to do.

Ring! It was time for class.

"Seats, everyone," said Mrs. Case.

I walked over to my desk and sat down. Vanessa smiled at me. I smiled back. I had my best friend Grace back. Courtney was talking to me again. Everything was going to be okay.

"Good morning," I said to Vanessa.

"Morning!" she replied. She looked happy that someone had talked to her today. I didn't think that was right.

Vanessa didn't deserve to be ignored. Being polite to her didn't hurt Courtney or anyone else. I wasn't going to be mean to anyone. That just wasn't me. And I like the person I am.

Ending 3: New Friends

What am I going to do? I have no idea. But I do know this. I am not going to let Courtney boss me around anymore. Courtney doesn't like the new girl, but that's her problem. That doesn't mean that Vanessa and I can't be friends.

I sit right next to Vanessa all day. I can't ignore her, can I? I shook my head. No, that wasn't right. If we sat next to each other, why did we have to act like strangers?

I knew how it felt to be the new girl. Courtney and her friends were treating her like they had treated me. It was just like the third grade all over again.

But two years had gone by. I was in the fifth grade now. And they were treating her—and me—as if we didn't matter. Making fun of our hair. Talking about us to other people. Making us feel unwelcome. That wasn't right.

I looked at Grace. She looked back. She was still my friend. Her grandmother was sick, that was the problem. That was why she was ignoring me. She didn't hate me like everyone else did. She was just upset about her grandmother. I knew what that was like. It was scary when someone you loved got sick. What if she died?

I shook my head. No, no, no. I wasn't going to think about that. My grandmother got better. Grace's grandmother would get better too.

"It's almost time for class," said Grace.

"Let's go in," I replied. We walked into the school and past the office. Mrs. Thatcher was by the door. When she saw us, she came out into the hall.

"Thanks for helping Grace with the flag, Sara," she said.

"That's what friends are for," I said. I put my arm around Grace.

"How is the new girl doing?" asked Mrs. Thatcher.

"Vanessa?" I said.

Mrs. Thatcher nodded.

"She sits next to me in class and at lunch," I said. I decided then and there that we would sit with Grace today. Why not? Grace was my old friend and Vanessa was my new one. We would sit in our regular spot and Vanessa would sit with us.

"I knew we could count on you," said Mrs. Thatcher. "Now off to class you go. It's almost time for the bell to ring."

"Okay," I said. Grace just smiled.

We walked down the hallway past the cafeteria. Things would be different today. Yesterday Vanessa and I had to sit with another class—on the other side of the cafeteria. Just to get away from them! And Courtney talked about me loudly. She made sure I heard it all. She wanted to embarrass me. Why was she so cruel?

Wait a minute. Why was I trying to be friends with someone who was so cruel? Grace was my friend. She was a real friend. She had troubles of her own, big troubles. That's why she ignored me before, but I understand that.

I remember when my grandmother got sick. I was so upset. I couldn't eat. I couldn't sleep. It was like a nightmare, but I was still awake.

I understood what it felt like to be the new girl, too.

Grace and I walked into class. I looked at Vanessa. Her desk was still next to mine. Vanessa was sitting in the back of the class, all by herself. No one was talking to her. That just wasn't right.

I looked over at Grace. I couldn't make her grandmother better, but I could be a friend. I could do that.

Grace treated me like a friend when she didn't really know me. It took a long time to get the popular kids to talk to me. And now they weren't. Just like she did before, Grace talked to me when no one else would.

I could do the same for Vanessa. What was that saying? Pass it on. It was on the bumper sticker of that car in the carpool line this morning. Pass it on. Yes, that was what I was going to do.

Grace helped me when I was the new girl. Now it was up to me to help Vanessa. She was

the new girl now. Yes, that's what I would do. I would pass it on. I would treat Vanessa like a friend.

"Will you please come with me?" I asked Grace.

"Sure, let's go," she replied with a shrug.

We quickly walked to the back of the class. I led us right over to Vanessa's desk. She didn't even look up when we stopped right next to it.

"Hi, Vanessa," I said. She finally glanced up. She seemed surprised to see Grace standing there. Grace hadn't talked to anyone but Lexi in days.

"This is my friend, Grace," I said. "We were wondering if you would sit with us at lunch today. At the fifth grade tables."

"I'd like that," said Vanessa.

"So would I," said Grace.

There, it was settled. We wouldn't talk about Grace's grandmother. We wouldn't talk about Courtney either. We would just get to know one another. My old friend, my new friend, and me.

That day at lunch, the other kids stared at us. They didn't laugh or tease, but they weren't very welcoming either. Still, Grace, Vanessa, and I had fun. We laughed and joked. Vanessa was really funny.

Eventually, everyone started giving Vanessa a chance. Even Courtney gave in and talked to her. But Grace and I were her best friends. We did everything together. When Grace's grandmother got better, we all visited her and brought her homemade cards.

I was glad I hadn't let Courtney keep me from being nice to Vanessa. If I had, I wouldn't have made a new friend. I wouldn't have become one of the Three Musketeers of Meadows Elementary School!

It is good to have friends and treat people the way I want to be treated. I hope there are more people in the world that are talking to new kids and making them feel welcome!

Write Your Own Ending

There were three endings to choose from in *The New Girl*. Did you find the ending you wanted from the story? Or did you want something different to happen?

Now it is your turn! Write an ending you would like to happen for Sara, Vanessa, Grace, and Courtney. Be creative!

5/14